THE KITCHEN HOUSE

I0821353

How Yesterday's Black Women Created Today's Most Popular & Famous American Foods!

by Carole Marsh

Black Jazz, Pizzazz & Razzmatazz™

Graphic Design: Cecil Anderson

Gallopade is proud to be a member of these educational organizations and associations:

The National School Supply and Equipment Association
The National Council for the Social Studies
Association for Supervision and Curriculum Development
Museum Store Association
Association of Partners for Public Lands

Black Jazz, Pizzazz, & Razzmatazz Books

Our Black Heritage Coloring Book

The Big Book of African American Activities

Black Heritage GameBook: Keep Score! Have Fun!
Find out how much you already know—and learn lots more!

Black Trivia: The African American Experience A-to-Z!

Celebrating Black Heritage:
20 Days of Activities, Reading, Recipes, Parties, Plays, and More!

Mini Timeline of Awesome African American Achievements and Events

"Let's Quilt Our African American Heritage & Stuff It Topographically!"

The Best Book of Black Biographies

The Color Purple & All That Jazz!: African American Achievements in the Arts

"Out of the Mouths of Slaves": African American Oral History

Black Business: African American Entrepreneurs & Their Amazing Success!

Other Carole Marsh Books

Meet Shirley Franklin: Mayor of Atlanta!

African American Readers—Many to choose from!

Table of Contents

A Word From the Author

Dear Readers,

The truth of the matter is that America's food and cooking heritage is not all that pretty. After all, millions of Africans were enslaved to work on sugar plantations to satisfy the European craving for sweets. Indeed, the growing sugar industry from about 1550 on, was one of the great forces behind the expansion of slavery and helped ease the introduction of slave labor to the cotton plantations of the American colonies.

In the homes of the well-to-do throughout the American South, cooking was done by slaves, primarily women. So, it is a fact that, at one time, black women formed the largest body of professional cooks in America! Many were not only outstanding cooks, but skilled culinary artisans. These talented women (and later, men) took the foodstuffs available in the New World, added ingredients secretly brought with them from Africa, and invented wonderful new recipes that have endured to this day. The appropriate names for many of our finest colonial recipes might be more accurately called Old Ebba's Lemon Chess Pie than Lady Charleston's Elegant Lemon Pie!

Not only were the "receipt books" of those days filled with delicious dishes, they were also chock full of ingenious household hints related to dying homespun, food preservation, making paint, tree cultivation, cures for "auges & fevers," washing silk stockings, or getting rid of the bugs that plagued even the most elegant plantations.

With courage and confidence, even in desperation, and often despite resources, our fore-gourmets made endless creative culinary contributions which endure—deliciously so—until today: a mere 400 hungry years later!

Carole Marsh

P.S.: All recipes come from authentic sources. Many include the original language and cooking terminology. Parents/teachers: Many recipes have been simplified so that children can prepare them at home or in the classroom. A crockpot is suitable for most boiled dishes; a toaster oven can be used for most baking.

The Kitchen House

Plantations were not merely houses, but little planetary systems around which a whole set of people and buildings orbited—schoolhouse, stables, henhouse, dairy, dovecote, smokehouse, springhouse, slave quarters, ice house, and kitchen. Usually a short distance from the manor, the kitchen was full of the cook's wares: pots, kettles, waffle irons, swinging cranes, bake ovens, scales, iron firedogs holding rotating spits. This was the spot in which southern cooking had its inspiration. The demand was great: often as many as 50, even 70, people would be on hand for a meal!—Marshall Fishwick, in the American Heritage Cookbook, 1964

The "kitchen house" was called a house because it often was a building separate from the main house used strictly for cooking. It was usually not very large—just big enough for a large table for cutting and preparing food, rolling pie crust dough, and all the other things that had to be done by hand. There was always a large fireplace, which was kept burning hot with coals—winter and summer! Today, we would recognize some of the kitchen tools. They might look old-fashioned, but we would know a colonial whisk or frying pan or flour sifter if we saw it. However, other tools might look a little more like weapons or surgeon's tools and we would have to guess what they were used for!

Being the "cook" was hard, hot, long, and tiring work. However, at least the cook had a chance to be creative. Sometimes that was tough—perhaps you had to figure out how to feed 50 people with little more to work with than leftover meat and rice. Other times, you might be able to invent a delicious new recipe, that even if never written down, would be so popular it would continue to be prepared for hundreds of years! So important were the kitchen equipment and the recipes that they were often kept under lock, with the mistress of the plantation guarding the only keys!

Early cooks, black and white, learned a great deal from the Native Americans who had been growing corn and vegetables such as squash and pompions (pumpkins) in the New World for a long time.

Cabbage Heads!

If you didn't have anything else to eat, at least you could probably eat cabbage! That's another way of saying that slave cooks, and the black and white families they fed, often ate a lot of what they could grow a lot of. Pilgrim women had brought cabbage seeds with them to plant in the New World. While in the New England states, cabbage was made into sauerkraut. In the colonial states, it was usually just boiled and served plain or with as many spices as you could round up.

Stewed Cabbage

1 head of cabbage
3-4 slices of fatback*

Cut up cabbage into quarters, then break the quarters up with your hands. Fry down the meat in a cast-iron dutch oven. Now put cabbage in the pot and fry it down about 10 minutes (turning often.) Salt and pepper to taste and add 1 cup of water. Bring it to a boil and then put on the lid and cook 20 minutes on medium low heat.

While you cook, sing:

* Fatback = a salty piece of pork meat with fat attached.

Boil that cabbage down boy,
boil that cabbage down
Bat your eyes til the crick done rise,
But boil that cabbage down!

Hoppin' John!

Many slaves lived on coastal Carolina plantations where they raised rice. This was hard work but rice was so valuable a crop that one brand of rice was named Carolina Gold! When cooked, this rice became large, fluffy kernels with a nutty flavor. Early cooks learned to combine rice with black-eyed peas to make a popular dish called Hoppin' John. It was often served on New Year's Day. A shiny new dime was put into the pot and the lucky person who got the coin was supposed to enjoy good luck all year long.

Rice was the colony's great staple, served with meat, shellfish & used to make breads, biscuits, flour, puddings & cakes.

Hoppin' John

- 1 cup raw cowpeas*
- 4 cups water
- 2 teaspoons salt
- 1 cup raw rice
- 4 slices bacon fried with 1 medium onion, chopped

Boil peas in salted water until tender. Add peas and 1 cup of the pea liquid to rice, bacon (with grease) and onion. Put in rice steamer or double-boiler and cook for 1 hour or until rice is thoroughly done.

* Cowpeas = an old name for black-eyed peas

Other rice dishes included red beans and rice cooked with ham and a rice pudding dessert made with milk and sugar.

Great Sufferin' Succotash!

The Native American Indians grew corn long before the colonists and slaves came to the New World. However, it didn't take long for the newcomers to learn the value of the crop called "maize." From corn came meal for cornbread, corn pone, ash cakes, Johnny cakes, and "hush puppies." In addition to boiling corn and eating in "on the cob," cooks "puffed" corn kernels to make hominy or ground dried corn to make grits. Soon, corn dishes were created such as corn pudding and corn "oysters" (a corn fritter.)

Beans were another early American crop that colonial cooks, black and white, learned to use in many dishes. A popular dish combining corn and beans was called succotash, a healthy, inexpensive, easy to prepare one-dish meal many people still enjoy today!

Succotash

- 1 c. fresh corn (cooked)
- 1 c. fresh lima or butterbeans
- 1 c. fresh cooked tomatoes chopped
- 1/3 c. of salt
- meat or bacon
- 1/3 c. onions (chopped)

Fry meat. Mix everything together. Add enough water to cover the bottom of the pot. Bring to a boil and serve.

Hush puppies got their name from when soldiers would throw corn balls to their dogs to keep them from barking and giving away their position.

Eatin' Goober Peas!

One of the most important food items slaves brought with them from Africa to America was the peanut. In the New World, peanuts were first planted as feed for pigs. However, black slave cooks "borrowed" some of this pig feed to help feed themselves and their children. The dishes they created were so delicious that the plantation mistress was soon asking for the recipes to be prepared for everyone.

In Africa, peanuts were served fresh from the garden as a vegetable. In America, peanuts were used to make soup, stuffings for a goose or duck, pies, breads, candy, and cake. Peanuts were also known as groundnuts, goobers, or goober peas. Later in history, George Washington Carver, an African American scientist whose parents were both slaves, spent years at the Tuskegee Institute in Alabama experimenting with using peanuts to make cheese, milk, coffee, flour, and many other things!

So, the next time you enjoy a peanut butter and jelly sandwich, you know who to thank!

Boiled Peanuts

A good after-school snack!

If they're green: put them in a pot, add water to cover and a tablespoon of salt. Boil 2 or 3 hours until the hardest ones are tender. If they're dried: put them in a pot of water and bring them to a boil. Cut off the fire, and let them stand overnight or at least 6-8 hours. Then boil in salted water for 4 to 5 hours, until the nut inside the shell is tender. NOTE: Some people are allergic to peanuts!

Okra, Roux, and Gumbo!

Okra, related to the hibiscus plant, is native to tropical Africa and Asia and was cultivated by the Egyptians, who brought it to America with the slaves. It was once ground to make a coffee substitute!

Early American black women used okra to thicken soups and stews. Later, they learned to mix flour and butter to form a paste called a roux *(pronounced ROO)* which turned dark brown and made a delicious base for many dishes. This roux was the basis for making a type of soup called gumbo. Gumbo also includes fish or seafood, rice, tomatoes, and spices. It is especially popular today in Louisiana where it is part of the traditional Cajun or Creole cuisine.

Early cooks learned to use the Choctaw Indians' powdered sassafras leaves (later called filé gumbo) to add flavor and texture to dishes.

Fried Okra

1 lb. of fresh okra (cut in 1/4-inch rounds)
1 &1/2 cups corn meal
1/3 cup oil
Salt, pepper

Salt and pepper okra, then shake it in a brown paper sack with 1 and 1/2 cups of meal till okra is all covered. Heat skillet very hot with 1/3 cup of oil. Put in okra and fry to golden brown (12 minutes or thereabout). Remove from skillet and lay okra on paper towel to absorb excess oil. Serve hot. Enough for 4 hungry folks.

Collards and Greens!

Especially in the winter, women in the kitchen house struggled to find enough healthy food to cook for the many people that made up the plantation. "Greens" of all types were boiled to be eaten, hopefully, with some corn pone or other bread. Collards, especially, tasted even better after the first frost. Just boiled with water, they would taste pretty bad, but black cooks doctored them up with herbs, spices, seasonings, and when available, a hog jowl (jaw) for extra flavor. This "mess of greens" was drained and the green juice (called "pot likker") was poured over bread. Today we call this type of cooking "soul food," and it is still much-admired, just as delicious, and still as healthy as it was 400 years ago when it was often eaten just so you wouldn't starve to death!

Did you know Eastern North Carolina grows the most delicious collards in the whole world?

Collard Greens

Wash your collards 3 or 4 times in fresh water, draining them each time. (Gritty collards are yucky!) Then strip the leafy part from the stems and throw the stems out. (I feed mine to my bunny rabbits, Snowshoe and Earmuff!) In a large pot, fry down 1 lb. of fatback, thick bacon, or ham chunks till brown. Add the cleaned collards. Stir and fry all this until collards start to wilt. Add 2 cups of water and cook until tender. Add more water if necessary. Some people like a spoon of sugar in the water to sweeten the greens. Stir frequently on medium heat so they don't burn. Serve with cornbread. Save the juice in the pot to pour over the bread!

Collards, collards, collards, Boiling in the pot,
With backbone, ham or fat back, And pepper red and hot.
Of all the vegetables, leafy and green, Collards are definitely the queen!

Colleen Bunting
Scotland Neck, North Carolina, in Leaves of Green The Collard Poems

Soups and Stews!

When you had a lot of folks to feed, and perhaps only a pinch of this and a smidgen of that, and especially during the cold wintertime, soups and stews could be found boiling in a big black kettle over the hot fireplace of the kitchen house. A basic soup or stew was made with any pieces of meat, fish, or bird you could round up, along with vegetables, rice, herbs and spices, and broth, cooked until hot and boiling, then simmered until time to serve.

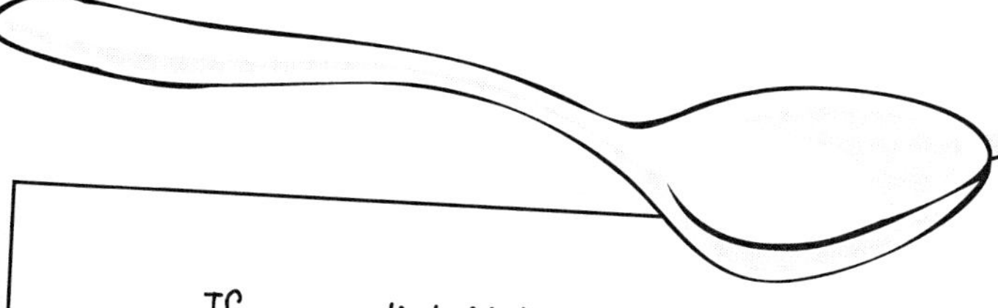

Simple Soup

If you didn't have anything else to eat, you could often prepare a soup from little of nothing. Crumble bread into a bowl of warm milk. Salt, pepper, and eat with a spoon. My grandmother used to feed this to me when I had a tummyache. Sing: *Hooka tooka my soda crackers?/Does yer Mammy chaw tobaccer?/If yer Mammy chaw tobaccer/Then Hooka tooka my soda cracker?*

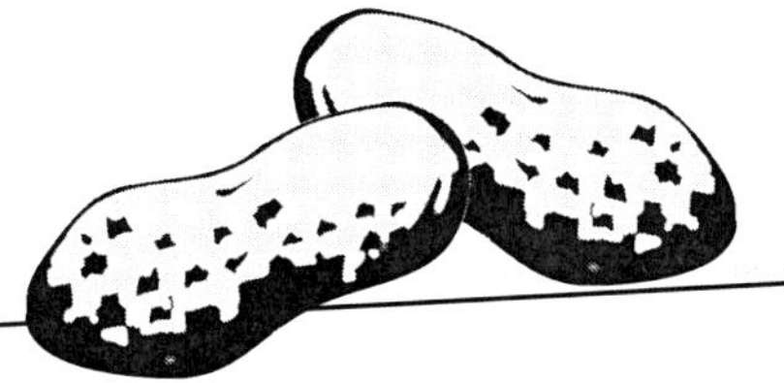

Tuskegee Peanut Soup

Sauté 4-5 minced scallions (green onions) in oil 2-3 minutes. Stir in 1/2 cup peanut butter and 3 tablespoons of flour; blend until smooth. Off the heat, stir in 2 cups of chicken stock; return to heat and let mixture thicken. Add 1/2 cup cream. Season with salt, cayenne pepper, and savory. Serve hot. Note: Some people are allergic to peanuts.

Possum Pie!

Meat was a welcome sight in the kitchen house! A good hunting trip might contribute rabbit, possum, quail, pheasant, or other wild game to that night's supper. Stop and think how different it was to prepare dinner when you did not start with "store-bought" styrofoam packages of meat, but instead, had to skin a rabbit or ring the neck of a squawking chicken!

Roast Possum

Possum should be cleaned as soon as possible after shooting. It should be hung for 48 hours and is then ready to be skinned and cooked. The meat is light-colored and tender. Excess fat may be removed, but there is no strong flavor or odor contained in the fat.

- 1 possum
- 1 onion, chopped
- 1 tbls. fat
- 1 c. breadcrumbs
- 1 hard-boiled egg, chopped
- 1 tsp. salt
- Water

Rub possum with salt and pepper. Brown onion in fat. Add possum liver and cook until tender. Add breadcrumbs, egg, salt, and water. Mix thoroughly and stuff possum. Truss like a fowl. Put in roasting pan with bacon across back and pour quart of water into pan. Roast uncovered in moderate oven (350 degrees) until tender, about 2 and 1/2 hours.

Old Wives' Tales

- There's only one thing to serve with possum–sweet potatoes.
- You only can eat possum in the winter.

Rabbit Pie

Rabbits should be decapitated and dressed immediately after shooting. After skinning, wipe the carcass with a cloth dipped in scalding water to remove loose hair. Cut rabbit into serving pieces. Soak in equal parts of vinegar and water for 12 - 24 hours. Drain and wipe dry. Sprinkle with salt and pepper and dredge with flour. Sear quickly in frying pan till golden. Add water to cover and simmer slowly in covered pot for 1 & 1/2 hours. Add 2 onions, 2 medium-sized carrots and 2 or 3 potatoes, all cut in pieces. Cook until vegetables are done. Thicken with flour. Cook in a greased baking dish in a hot oven until bubbling. Cover with biscuit dough and return to oven to bake till dough is done.

Candy and Cookies!

Sweets were not common in the kitchen house. Sugar, when available, was valued and used sparingly. It was often stored under lock and key! However, sweets were made using sugar substitutes such as honey, molasses, and other natural sweeteners. Benne (sesame) seeds were secretly brought to America on the slave ships by black women who had used them in their native cooking. Benne seed cookies and candy were made by black cooks in Charleston and other lowcountry South Carolina locations. They replenished their benne seeds by planting a few seeds at the far end of each row of cotton, for example, to harvest later. Freed slave cooks often continued to make benne candy, which was peddled on the streets of Charleston and Savannah to white people.

Groundnut Candy

1 qt. molasses
4 cups shelled peanuts, roasted
1 c. brown sugar
1/2 cup butter

Combine all ingredients except nuts, and boil for 1/2 hour over a slow fire. Then add the roasted and shelled peanuts and continue cooking for 15 minutes. Drop on lightly greased cookie sheet or on a piece of marble. Make little cakes of the candy and let harden. Note: some people are allergic to peanuts.

Benne-Seed Cookies

1 cup flour
1/4 tsp. salt
3/4 cup butter
2 eggs, beaten
1 tsp. vanilla extract
peanut oil
1/2 tsp. baking powder
2 cups brown sugar
3/4 cup benne(sesame) seeds

Preheat oven to 325 degrees. Sift flour, baking powder, and salt. Cream butter and add brown sugar; stir till fluffy. Beat in eggs and vanilla. In a large skillet, toast sesame seeds until taffy colored; add to batter. Oil a large cookie sheet. Drop batter by teaspoonfuls 1 and 1/2 inches apart. Bake in upper part of oven for 10 minutes. Let cookies cool 1 minute then scrape onto a rack to cool. Makes 6 dozen.

Breads and Biscuits!

Great black pans of breads of all types were always baking in the kitchen house. It might be shortnin' bread, beaten biscuits, sweet potato pone, cracklin cornbread, or dark, spicy gingerbread. Someone could always be found kneading dough on the big slab of table or in a worn, wooden bowl.

When there wasn't enough room for regular biscuits at the end of a pan, a rope biscuit was laid to fill out the space. It was called "the Booga Man." The smallest child got this mealtime treat.

Short'nin Bread

1 and 1/2 cups flour
1/4 lb. butter (soft)
1/4 cup light brown sugar

Cream the butter and sugar. Add the flour and mix thoroughly. Roll out quickly, about 1/2 inch thick, on a floured board. Use the lid to a fruit jar or a jelly glass to cut out your shapes. Place on greased-and-floured shallow pan and bake at 350 degrees for about 20 minutes.

Cracklin Corn Pone

1 cup milk (boiling)
2 cups cornmeal
1 tsp. baking powder
1/2 tsp. salt
2/3 cup cracklins, or 1 c. of pig skins
2 tbls. bacon drippings

Sift cornmeal, baking soda, and salt into a bowl. Then, pour enough boiling milk into this to make a stiff batter. Add the cracklins, or pig skins, and bacon drippings. Shape into pones in the palm of your hand or pour in a black skillet and bake at 425 degrees until golden. Make sure the skillet is well greased.

Cracklins are the skins and other pieces left after the rendering of pork fat at hog-killing time in the Fall after the first frost. *Pones* are small, oval shapes.

Pies and Puddings!

When fruit trees were in season, it was time to fill flaky dough crusts with apples or other fruit. Pies were also made with rhubarb (it looks like red celery!), sweet potatoes, eggs, milk, and many other ingredients. "Cobblers" were baked in the fire in big, black pots. Surely the kitchen house cooks could not resist "sampling" their treats... just to make sure they tasted just right.

Fresh Peach Cobbler

12 peaches
2 tbls. flour
1/2 tsp. baking powder
1/2 cup milk or cream
juice of 1/2 lemon
1 tbls. sugar
1 and 1/2 cups flour
7 tbls. butter
1 egg
1/4 cup sugar

Preheat oven to 425 degrees. Butter a deep dish casserole. Slice peaches and sprinkle with lemon juice; arrange in pan. Mix flour and sugar and sprinkle over fruit. Dot fruit with 2 tbls. butter. Sift flour, baking powder, 1 tbls. of sugar, and cut in 5 tbls. of butter; mix lightly. Beat egg with milk or cream. Stir into flour until mixture is smooth. Drop in small mounds over fruit. Bake for 30 minutes. Makes 8 servings.

Indian Pudding

5 cups milk, divided
1/2 cup yellow cornmeal
3/4 tsp. ground nutmeg
2/3 cup dark molasses
3/4 tsp. ground cinnamon
1/3 cup sugar
1 tsp. salt
1/4 cup butter

Preheat oven to 300 degrees. Grease 1-1/2 quart baking dish. Heat 4 cups milk. Stir in molasses, sugar, cornmeal, cinnamon, nutmeg, salt and butter. Cook, stirring constantly, till mixture thickens. Pour into baking dish. Pour remaining cup of cold milk carefully over top; do not stir. Bake 3 hours without stirring. Serve warm with cream, ice cream or hard sauce. Makes 8 servings.

Indian Pudding was served in all the original colonies. It was often precooked, then baked in the dutch oven with breads and pies.

Sweet Potatoes: I Yam (Not!) What I Yam

Sweet potatoes look, are prepared like, and generally taste like "yams," but are not even related! However, yams were brought to the New World by slaves. During hunting season, roast possum and sweet potatoes was a favorite meal. Either yams or sweet potatoes will work in the following recipes.

Sweet Potato Pone

4 cups grated raw sweet potatoes
2 cups molasses or dark corn syrup
1 cup warm milk
1 c. brown sugar
1 tsp. cinnamon

Mix ingredients; pour into greased baking dish. Bake in moderate oven until crust forms on top (about 45 minutes.) Serve hot with unsweetened cream, plain or whipped.

Yam Pudding

Take a pound of Yams boil'd dry, beat it fine in a mortar with a pound Butter til it Puffs, take ten eggs, half the whites, beat them with a pound sugar and half a pint of wine with Spice, the juice of a lemon with a little of the rine, and some slices of citron laid on the top. –

Eliza Lucas Pinckney
Rect. Book No. 2
Charleston, South Carolina, 1756

Long potatoes were the colonial term for sweet potatoes.

Pickles and Such!

Cucumbers were generally an easy crop to grow in the sandy soil of plantation lands. They were primarily used to make a variety of types of pickles. African women were familiar with spices and brought many of them to the New World. These were often used to pep up the pickles!

Ice Tomato Pickles

3 lbs. sugar
1 tsp. cloves
1 tsp. allspice
1 tsp. mace
2 pints vinegar
1 tsp. ginger
1 tsp. celery seed
1 tsp. cinnamon

Slice 7 pounds of green tomatoes, and soak in lime water for 24 hours. (Use three cups lime to 2 gallons water.) Drain. Soak in fresh water for 48 hours, changing water every hour. Drain.

Then make syrup of above ingredients. Bring to boil and pour over tomatoes. Let stand overnight. Next morning, boil one hour and seal while hot. Makes very crispy pickles.

Bread & Butter Pickles

1 qt. sliced cucumbers
1 large onion, sliced
3/4 cup sugar
3/4 cup vinegar (white)
1 tsp. salt
1/4 tsp. dry mustard
1/4 tsp. tumeric
1 tsp. mustard seeds

Wash and slice cucumbers. Place cucumbers and onions in a large pot with everything else. Bring to a boil, stirring occasionally. Pour into sterilized jars, making certain liquid covers cucumbers. Seal. They will be ready to eat in 2 or 3 days.

Black Food in the White House

When Rosalynn was visiting the White House, some of our staff asked the chef and cooks if they thought that they could prepare the kind of meals which we enjoyed in the South, and the cook said, "Yes, Ma'am, we've been fixing that kind of food for the servants for a long time!"—entry in President Jimmy Carter's White House diary, January 20, 1977

It went something like this. The Indians and the slaves and the new colonists shared all types of food and cooking ideas over time, and soon, dishes with these historic backgrounds began to be served in the White House.

Since most black women could not write, they had no way to record their recipes. In fact, like many good cooks, they did not really need a written record to repeat the making of a particular dish. That was part of their wonderful creativity—they made it up—often improving it again and again—each time, using new ideas and ingredients until they settled upon their most popular method for preparing a favorite food.

Some colonial women did record recipes based on these types of dishes, and they were shared far and wide, often ending up on the table of the president of the United States! Such dishes might include an oyster dressing stuffed turkey, eggnog, or homemade relishes.

The third U.S. president, Thomas Jefferson, took his slave cook to Paris where he was taught the finest French cooking. He became a first-class chef and changed American cooking by bringing back glamorous recipes and new foods such as ice cream, spaghetti, and waffles.

American presidents and their friends were fond of hunting. In the South, it was traditional for African American boys and men to tend to the outdoor cooking (a barbecue!) of wild game. Many of them became experts at cooking. Later, black men often became chefs at private clubs, fine restaurants, and yes, even at the White House!

Cornucopia

Read this and see if it makes your mouth water! What a difference this "groaning board" of food must have seemed to the blacks. Even though they generally didn't get to eat this fine food, the black cooks were almost always the ones to prepare it. In fact, slaves were often fed spoiled meat and weevil-filled bread. However, on some plantations, slaves were fed so well that they truly missed their former meals after they were freed. Even though it would have been hard, hot work for the kitchen house cooks, perhaps they often took some pleasure in their chance to experiment and create with such a variety of foods.

The close-fisted stinginess that fed the poor slave on coarse cornmeal and tainted meat... wholly vanished on approaching the sacred precincts of the Great House itself... Immense wealth and its lavish expenditures filled the Great House with all that could please the eye or tempt the taste. Fish, flesh, and fowl, were here in profusion. Chickens of all breeds, ducks of all kinds... guinea fowls, turkeys, geese, and peafowls... partridges, quails, pheasants, pigeons. ... Beef, veal, mutton, and venison. ... The teeming riches of the Chesapeake Bay, its rock perch, drums, crocus, trout, oysters, crabs and terrapin, were drawn hither to adorn the glittering table. The dairy, too, ... poured its rich donations of fragrant cheese, golden butter, and delicious cream to heighten the attractions of the gorgeous, unending round of feasting. ... The tender asparagus, the crispy celery, and the delicate cauliflower, eggplants, beets, lettuce, parsnips, peas, and French beans, early and late; radishes, cantaloupes, melons of all kinds; and the fruits of all climes and of every description, from the hardy apples of the North to the lemon and orange of the South, culminated at this point. Here were gathered figs, raisins, almonds, and grapes from Spain, wines and brandies from France, teas of various flavor from China, and rich, aromatic coffee from Java...

Frederick Douglass
Life and Times of Frederick Douglass, 1892

Frederick Douglass was a slave who became a free newspaperman, U.S. marshal, and Minister to Haiti.

Diamondback terrapin (turtle) was once so abundant in Maryland, it was served to slaves as often as three times a week!

Grits and Hominy!

In addition to the use of corn as meal, southerners converted it into hominy and grits. Both were made from corn, but the grains went through a soaking process which removed the husk (not the shuck) from the grain. Hominy consisted of whole grain corn boiled and eaten as a vegetable. When hominy grains were dried, ground into a coarse meal, and boiled, the dish was called grits.

Sam Bowers Hilliard
Hog Meat and Hoecake, 1972

Grits with Country Ham & Red-Eye Gravy

6 (1/4 inch thick) slices country ham
1/4 cup margarine
1/4 cup firmly packed brown sugar
1/2 cup strong black coffee
Sprig of fresh mint

Cut gashes in fat to keep ham from curling. Sauté ham in margarine in a heavy skillet over low heat until light brown, turning several times. Remove ham from skillet and keep warm.

Stir sugar into pan drippings; cook over low heat until sugar dissolves, stirring constantly. Add coffee to pan drippings, stirring well. Simmer gravy 5 minutes and keep warm.

Journey Cakes

Journey cakes got their name because they served travelers as a quick food for snacking along the way. They were also called Johnny Cakes or Jonny Cakes. This is an old recipe, made from hominy.

"Take a pint of Hominy cold mash it and mix well with a gill fine flower then mix 6 Spoonsfull of milk and spread it on your board and spread a little milk over it as you put it down to bake. This quantity for 2 middlesized Journey cakes."

Soul Food!

What happened to black cooks after the slaves were freed? The women often cooked for their own families, or cooked for white families. They truly got little recognition for the contribution that they had made to the basic American foods that are still known and loved today. As the women continued to experiment with their cooking, they developed a form of black cuisine called "soul food." These dishes are still based on the traditional slave cooking, using meats, rice, cornmeal, sweet potatoes or yams, and seasonings and spices. Today, such recipes are highly-prized. Many entrepreneurs, black and white, have opened successful restaurants serving "soul food."

Many freed African American men also found a career in cooking. Some cooked for large plantations, private clubs, or in fine restaurants. Many of the best of the public cooks were black, male, and very well-trained. Some became chefs in the dining cars on the great cross-country passenger trains. Others headed up the galleys (kitchens) of the great steamships of the rivers and the oceans.

Today, so-called "soul food" is no longer considered the lowly food of poor plantation life and slave quarters. Variations of soul food can be found in the finest restaurants... and is often very expensive!

Soul Food: . . . "A type of cooking made necessary by the environment in which southern blacks lived" is the phrase one soul food restaurateur used to describe his cuisine.

Evan Jones
American Food, 1974

All But the Squeal!

Pork eventually became an important source of meat in the kitchen house. Hogs were often raised on the plantation, along with the cotton, rice, or vegetables. It was said that a pig was so valuable that every bit was used "except the squeal"!

From pork, you could get bacon, ribs, ham hocks, hog jowl, sausage, pig's feet, and many other "delicacies." You could also get lard (fat) for cooking. Even the intestines were used as casings for the sausage!

A ham was often a special feast saved for a holiday such as Christmas. The ham itself would have been served on a platter to the plantation family. The slave quarters usually would only get the leftover skin and pieces (called *chitlins*) to use to flavor their "mess of greens" or corn pone.

Pork in Apple Cider Sauce

- 1 pound boneless pork, cut into bite-sized strips
- 1 tbls. cooking oil
- 1 cup apple cider
- 1/4 cup chopped onion
- 1 medium apple, cored and coarsely chopped
- 2 cups hot cooked rice
- 4 tsp. cornstarch
- 1 tbls. brown sugar
- 1/2 tsp. salt
- 1/4 tsp. ground cinnamon
- 2 tbls. vinegar

In large saucepan, brown pork strips in hot oil; drain fat. Add 1/2 cup cider and onion, bring to boil; reduce heat, cover and simmer 40 minutes until meat is tender. In bowl combine cornstarch, brown sugar, salt and cinnamon. Blend in remaining cider and vinegar. Add to pork mixture with apple. Cook and stir till mixture is thick and bubbly, then 2 minutes more. Serve over rice. Serves 4.

Oysters and Fish!

Back in the days when the colonists and slaves first came to the New World, they discovered what the Native American Indians knew—that the oysters were as large as the forearm of a man! Fish of all types, oysters, clams, crabs, eel, and many others were plentiful in the rivers and the tidal creeks. Fishing was less a popular pastime than a necessity. Kitchen house cooks were experts at preparing all types of fish and seafood.

Pyckled Oisters

"Oisters, some very great, and some small, some round, and some of a long shape: they are found both in salt water and brackish, and those that we had out of salt water are far better than the other as in our countrey." Thomas Harriot, *A Briefe & True Repot of the New World*

- 1 quart oysters
- 1/2 cup vinegar
- 1/2 cup oyster liquor (juice)
- Whole black peppers and cloves

Cook spices in vinegar and liquor. When hot, add oysters and cook till they curl. Serve hot or cool.

Pine Bark Stew

The name comes from the fuel used for cooking the stew over an open fire. Pine bark burns for hours, providing extremely slow heat. A few oak sticks add sparkle and crackle.

- 1 pound bacon
- 12 medium potatoes, peeled and sliced
- 12 medium onions, sliced
- 12 servings bigmouth bass, broam or red breast, cleaned
- Boiling salted water
- 2 teaspoons curry powder

Cook bacon, remove and reserve. In bacon fat, place layer of 1/3 potatoes and onions in large pot. Cover with water. Simmer gently 10 minutes. Add a layer of 1/2 of fish; sprinkle with 1 teaspoon curry. Add 1/3 more potatoes, onions and rest of fish; sprinkle with curry. Add water to cover. Cook slowly until top layer of potatoes is cooked. Serve with sauce below over stew. Place bacon on top and serve with rice. 12 servings. Sauce: Mix 1/2 pound butter, 1/3 cup Worcestershire sauce, 1 cup catsup, 1/2 teaspoon red pepper and 1/2 teaspoon black pepper. Heat.

Something to Drink!

WATER, WATER, EVERYWHERE, BUT NARY A DROP TO DRINK? ONLY SLAVES, POOR WHITES, AND HARD-PRESSED FRONTIERSMEN DRANK WATER IN AMERICA'S EARLY DAYS. WITH ANY CHOICE, YOU DRANK RUM, SPRUCE BEER, CIDER, PEACH BRANDY, OR WHISKEY. WEALTHIER FAMILIES DRANK CIDER, PUNCH, SHRUB, BRANDY, CORDIALS, RATAFIAS, CLARET OR MADEIRA WINE. WHY? WATER WAS NOT ALWAYS FRESH OR TREATED AS IT IS TODAY. DRINKING ALMOST ANYTHING ELSE WAS TASTIER AND SAFER! KIDS DRANK MILK FROM A COW OR A GOAT. THIS MILK WAS NOT PASTEURIZED AS IT IS TODAY.

Lemons were not common in the New World, but when families could get some the kitchen house cook might make the following treat for the white plantation children.

Lemon Ice

3 cups cold water
3/4 cup corn syrup
2/3 cup fresh lemon juice
1 cup sugar
grated rind of 1 lemon

Put water, sugar, corn syrup and rind in saucepan and stir over medium heat till sugar dissolves. As soon as boils stop stirring, but boil for 5 minutes. Remove from heat and cool 15 minutes. Add lemon juice and cool thoroughly. Pour mixture into shallow trays and freeze until firm. Remove from trays and break into chunks in bowl and beat with electric mixer until mushy, getting air into ice. Put back into trays, cover with foil and freeze. Serve in chunks in chilled parfaits.

Tea made from herbs was supposed to be soothing to the stomach. This recipe may have been originally used by Indians before African American women began to prepare it in the kitchen houses.

Sassafras Bark Tea

4 pieces sassafras bark
5 teaspoons sugar
5 cups boiling water
Cream

Place pieces of rosy outer bark of sassafras root in enamelware pan or teapot. Pour boiling water over bark, cover container. Let steep in warm place for 5 minutes or till it is colored nicely. Strain into cups or hot teapot, add cream and serve with sugar to make a "saloop" or sweeten with honey. Serves 5.

Spice is Nice!

Early American Indian and colonial food was pretty bland until African American cooks introduced more herbs and spices into dishes. Having used such things back in their native country, they brought these ideas (and often seeds and plants) with them to the New World. Also, some slaves traveled through Caribbean islands where they picked up more ideas (and samples) for spicier foods. From Native Americans, they learned of local herbs to use in cooking.

Kitchen Pepper

"One ounce Ginger, half an ounce each pepper cinnamon cloves and Nutmeg, and 6 ounces of Salt. Mix it well and keep it dry."

Spicy Bouquet

In a net bag, place red peppers, cinnamon stick, whole nutmeg, whole peppercorns, mustard seeds, pieces of ginger or other spices. Tie tightly with string and let steep in pot with food until desired spiciness.

Sea Salt

Pour ocean water into shallow pan. Let water evaporate and scrape remaining salt into holder. Add a few grains of rice to keep salt from clumping together.

Condiments Galore!

Just as we enjoy condiments such as ketchup, mustard, and relish today, slave cooks invented all kinds of dishes to extend and enhance meals.

Walnut "Catchup"

While we think of ketchup as coming in a jar from the grocery store (or those little packs at McDonalds), somebody had to invent "catchup" first! (But how did they truly enjoy it without French fries?) Here is an old recipe for homemade ketchup made from nuts:

"Take 50 walnuts and bruise them well in a stone Mortar, put in three Pints of the best Vinegar and stir them every Day for 9 or 10 Days together, then strain through a Muslin and boil a quarter Hour with Mace, whole Pepper and Nutmeg."

Also popular were all types of pickled side dishes. Cooks might pickle cucumbers, melons, onions, or peaches. Some of these dishes were combinations of many things. If you wonder why it might take all day to make one dish, read this recipe!

Ats Jar Pucholilla

"Take Ginger one Pound, let it lie in Salt and Water one Night, then scrape it and cut it in thin slices, and put in a Bottle with dry Salt and let stand till the Rest of the Ingredients are ready. Take one Pound of Garlick divide it in Cloves and Past it. Take small Sticks of about two or three Inches long, and Rub them through the Cloves of Garlick. Salt them for three Day's, then wash them, and salt them again and let them stand three Day's longer, then salt them again and Put them in the Sun to Dry. Take Cabbages, cut them in Quarters and Salt them for three Day's then press the Water out of them, and put them in the Sun to Dry. Take long Pepper (cayenne), Salt it and dry it in the Sun, take 1/2 a pint of Mustard Seed, Wash it very Clean, and lay it to Dry. When it is very Dry bruise half of it in a Mortar, take an Ounce of Termarick (turmeric) bruised very Fine, put all these Ingredients into a Stone Jar, and put one Quart of the strongest Vinegar to 3 quarts of small. Fill the Jar 3 Quarters full, and supply it as often as you see Occasion. After the same Manner you may do Cucumbers, Melons, Plumbs, apples, Carrots, or any thing of that sort. They are to be put all together and you need never empty the Jar, but as the Season comes in dry the things and put them in, and fill them up in Vinegar. Be Careful, no Rain or Damp comes to them for that will make them Rott."

Food as Medicine!

OLD FASHIONED CURES (THAT MAY STILL WORK?)

One thing that black and white women could agree on was trying anything that might help cure some of the many ordinary or unusual aches, pains, illnesses, and diseases that plagued every plantation. Many of the "cures" that the black women brought from Africa were handed down in their new home. And of course the Indians and the English colonists had their own cures. Many of these are still handed down and used. While some people make fun of them, many are based on good common sense or experimentation and proof that they work.

Sometimes, even scientists find that the herbs or potions that seemed very unlikely to cure anything actually have some chemical that really does have healing powers and may even end up in a modern medicine!

When I was a child, my grandmother treated my ingrown fingernail with a "bread and milk poltice." She dipped my sore finger in milk and wrapped a small piece of bread around it, then covered it with a bandaid. The next morning, my finger was well! How do I explain that? I can't!

TO TREAT ULCERS: USE A PACK OF DOATY CORN AND SOME DOWN FROM A TURKEY'S RUMP!

YAUPON TEA WAS SUPPOSED TO HAVE ALMOST MAGICAL CURATIVE POWERS.

Thank You!

We owe a yummy "thank you" to African America women who brought the following to America, and helped create, invent, and improve the bland cooking that existed at that time.

FOODS BROUGHT TO AMERICA WITH THE SLAVES:

GUMBO	EGGPLANT	FIELD PEAS	SESAME SEEDS
YAMS	SORGHUM	BANANAS	PEANUTS
PEPPERS			

TECHNIQUES INVENTED:

- Beaten biscuits (beat 1/2 hour as a way to make the biscuits tender)
- Cooking "greens" with meat
- Spicing up soups and stews with hot pepper sauce

RECIPES DEVELOPED:

Filé Gumbo	Fried Chicken and Grits	Fried Catfish and Hominy
Journey Cakes	Mess o' Greens	Praline Candy

Mmm...mmm...mmm, Molasses!

Molasses was used as cattle feed because of its high carbohydrate content, which makes it a good fattener-upper. It was used in small amounts for tobacco curing and as the raw material for the yeast fermentation in making rum. Molasses was the only sugar form available to slaves and southern rural poor for many years. Molasses was also used to make gingerbread, in shoo-fly pie, and baked beans. Slaves were given blackstrap molasses, the bitter dregs left after three boilings of sugar cane. This is an old Christmas recipe for fruitcake made with molasses.

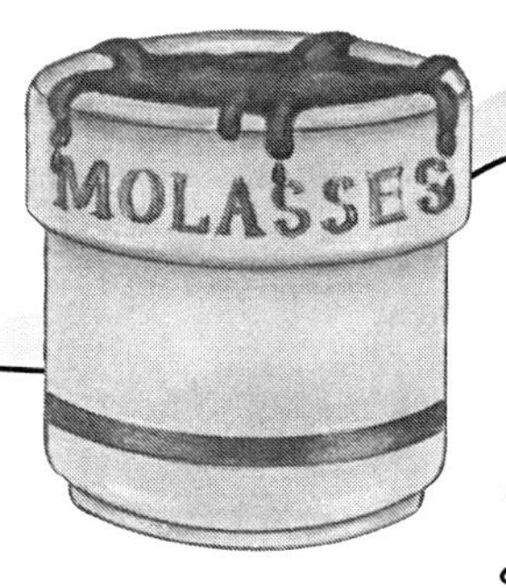

Molasses Fruitcake

1/4 cup butter
3/4 cup applesauce
1 teaspoon rum or brandy extract
2 and 1/2 cups plain flour
1 teaspoon baking powder
1/2 teaspoon ground nutmeg
1/2 teaspoon ginger
1 cup walnuts, coarsely chopped
8 ounces maraschino cherries, drained
3/4 cup molasses
Juice and grated rind of 1 orange
2 eggs
1 teaspoon baking soda
1/3 cup strong coffee
1/2 teaspoon cloves
1 cup raisins
1 and 1/2 teaspoons ground cinnamon

Cream butter and molasses until fluffy. Beat in applesauce, orange rind and juice, extracts, coffee and eggs.
Sift 2 cups of flour with other dry ingredients and spices. Add to molasses mixture and mix well. Toss fruit and nuts with remaining flour and fold into batter.
Grease a 9-inch tube pan. Line bottom with waxed paper. Pour batter into pan, and garnish with cherries and nuts. Bake at 325 degrees for 1 and 1/2 hours. Let stand in pan 20 minutes, then turn out and cool on rack. Icing: Cream 1/4 cup butter, softened, with 2 cups powdered sugar and 2 tablespoons cold coffee to smooth, spreading consistency.

Kitchen House Miscellany!

We Raise De Wheat

"We raise de wheat,
Dey gib us de corn;
We bake de bread,
Dey gib us de crust;
We sif de meal,
Dey gib us de huss;
We peel de meat,
Dey gib us de skin;
And dat's de way
Dey take us in;
We skim de pot,
Dey gib us de liquor
And say dat's good
Enough for us."
Anonymous slave song

Every August they would have a Big Meetin' and all the slaves that had died durin' the year, they would preach them a funeral that day. They would build a big Bush Arbor an' Old Miss would give us this and that and we would cook it up and everybody would take dinner an' they would come for miles, all around in wagons an' car's an' spread a big dinner.—*Slave narrative of Catherine Beale, aged 91 in 1929*

"When we lef de white folks we had nothing to eat. De blacks wait there at de Freedmen's Bureau and they give 'em hard tack, white potatoes, and saltpeter meat. Our white folks give us good things to eat, and I cried everyday at 12 o'clock to go home. ... I would say 'Papa le's go home, I want to go home. I don't like this sumpin' to eat.' He would say, 'Don't cry, honey, le's stay here, dey will sen' you to school.'"
—*Slave narrative of Sarah Harris*

Questions For Discussion

1. What if you came to a new land of new foods? (This might certainly happen to you in the future, in today's multi-national business world!) How would you feel? What foods would you miss that you left behind? What types of foods would you like to explore eating?

2. Cooking is a very creative art. It involves a lot of experimentation. Often there is no right or wrong (unless it burns the kitchen down!) Take the following list of ingredients: flour; sugar; milk; eggs; apples; spinach; chocolate; and one spice of your choice. Now, create your own recipe out of your imagination. You don't have to use all the ingredients, but you can't use any extra (except for the spice), because that's all you have to work with. Give your recipe a name. Share it aloud with your fellow students and see if they would eat it. Give a round of applause to the dish that "sounds" the best. Then, you might even want to try making a batch of it to sample. What would you do differently ncxt time?

3. Ask your parents or grandparents if you have any "family" recipes. Make a copy of them to keep for yourself. What dishes do you eat at home now that you think your children or grandchildren might ask you for a copy of in the future?

4. How would a plantation cook have made a colonial pizza? What ingredients would she use?

5. How healthy do you think the foods of back then sound? What about today's foods?

6. Write out a menu for a colonial meal that the slave cook might have prepared. Now make a list of all the steps to prepare it. (Remember, she had no can opener, electric stove, etc.)

Further Resources

Southern Food
by John Edgerton

New Orleans Recipes
by Mary Moore Bremer

Vibration Cooking
by Vetamae Grosvenor

American Food
by Evan Jones

The Negro Chef Cookbook
by Leonard E. Roberts

Hog Meat and Hoecake
by Sam Bowers Hilliard

American Heritage Cookbook
by Marshall Fishwick

The Taste of America
by John and Karen Hess

African American Kitchen: Food for Body and Soul
by George Erdosh

Glossary of Kitchen House Era Cooking Terms

ashcake: bread cooked in the fireplace

benne: sesame seeds

buckwheat: natural or unprocessed wheat

chitlins: pig intestines

cracklin: pig skin

filé: sassafras leaves

firedogs: the andirons in the fireplace where cooking pots might hang

fool: a type of dessert

goober: peanut

gumbs: stewed okra

hoecake: bread cooked on a hoe stuck into the fireplace

pinch: a measurement equalling an amount you could "pinch" between your fingers

pinebark: a type of stew cooked over a pine bark fire

pone: bread or cake

receipt: old word for recipe

roots: vegetables which grew in the ground

sassafras: sarsaparilla, a root used to make a drink like root beer

smidgen: a cooking measurement meaning "just a little bit"

yam: sweet potato

Index

There are so many awesome African American achievements and accomplishments in history.

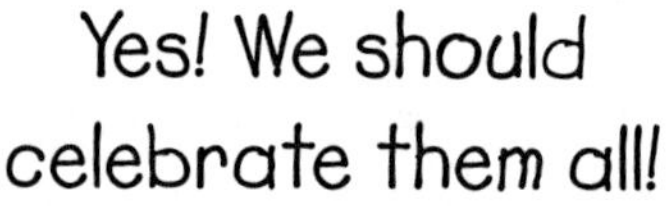